THE
GREAT
QUARTERBACK
SWITCH

READ ALL THE BOOKS

In The

New MATT CHRISTOPHER Sports Library!

New

MATT CHRISTOPHER

Sports Library

THE
GREAT
QUARTERBACK
SWITCH

NORWOOD HOUSE PRESS

CHICAGO, ILLINOIS

Norwood House Press

P.O. Box 316598
Chicago, Illinois 60631

For information regarding Norwood House Press, please visit our website
at: www.norwoodhousepress.com or call 866-565-2900.

Library of Congress Cataloging-in-Publication Data:
Christopher, Matt.
  The great quarterback switch / by Matt Christopher.
     p. cm.
  Summary: Twelve-year-old Michael, confined to a wheelchair after an
accident, uses mental telepathy to communicate football plays to his
quarterback twin brother Tom, then suddenly finds himself on the field in his
brother's place.
  ISBN-13: 978-1-59953-216-5 (library edition : alk. paper)
  ISBN-10: 1-59953-216-6 (library edition : alk. paper)
(1. Football—Fiction. 2. Twins—Fiction. 3. Brothers—Fiction. 4. People with
disabilities—Fiction. 5. Extrasensory perception—Fiction.) I. Title.
  PZ7.C458Gr 2008
  (Fic)—dc22   2008014996

Manufactured in the United States of America in North Mankato, Minnesota.
                              R142—092009

In memory of Mary Barnes

★ ★

The Eagles

*Bob Riley	80	End
*Stan Bates	81	End
Rick Howell	82	End
*Butch Bogger	70	Tackle
*Don Cleaver	72	Tackle
Stogey Snyder	75	Tackle
*Lumpy Harris	60	Guard
*Doug Morton	63	Guard
Phil Wheeler	65	Guard
*Jack Benson	50	Center
Mel Thomas	51	Center
*Vince Forelli	49	Fullback
Jason Tully	44	Fullback
*Jim Berry	31	Halfback
*Angie Costello	25	Halfback
Mick Doyle	21	Halfback
*Tom Curtis	11	Quarterback
Kirk Tyler	15	Quarterback
Frank Cotter		Coach

*First team

★ ★

"Do you think it's possible, Michael?"

*"Yes. If we both believe that it's possible, then I think it is.
But you must want it, just as much as I do."*

*"I do, Michael. I mean it. I really do.
I'd do anything to make you as happy as I am."*

"Thank you, Tom. Thank you very much."

★ ★

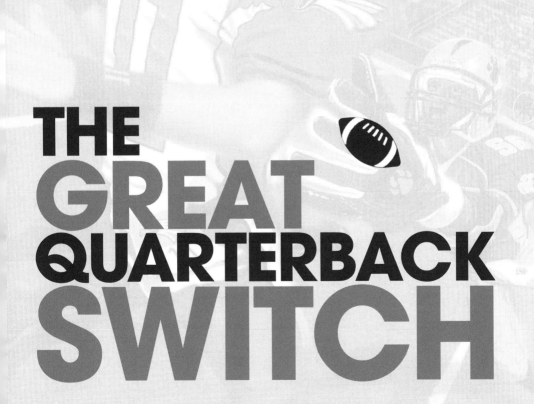

THE
GREAT
QUARTERBACK
SWITCH

T-forty-three drive!" Michael Curtis yelled, pressing his hands against the sides of his wheelchair in order to push himself up as far as he could. "T-forty-three drive, Tom!"

The Eagles had the ball on their own twenty-eight-yard line, and the T-43 drive was an effective play to try now, Michael thought. He hoped Tom thought so, too.

Rick Howell, the Eagles' substitute end, turned around on the bench next to Michael and smiled.

"Louder, Mike, and maybe Tom will hear

1

you," Rick said kiddingly, his blue eyes squinting against the late afternoon sun.

Michael blushed as he returned the smile. "Yeah," he said, "and so will the Colts. Why didn't you punch me?"

Rick shook his head. "Not me, kid. Tom told me about those biceps you've developed."

Michael's smile broadened. Ever since he had purchased a set of barbells, he had been kidded by his brother, Tom, about his bulging biceps. A few months ago Michael's arms had been as round and soft as uncooked sausages, but he'd firmed them up by working out.

Michael's attention shifted back to the game. He heard Tom calling signals, saw center Jack Benson snap the ball, then Tom take it and hand it off to fullback Vince Forelli, who charged straight ahead through the line. In the next play Tom handed the ball off to left halfback Jim Berry, who plunged through the right side of the line for a six-yard gain.

"Hey, how about that?" Michael cried, turning and slapping Rick on the shoulder. "Tom *did* call it!"

"Well, being twins, you guys could be tuned in on the same wavelength," Rick replied.

"You mean like ESP?" The dimple in Michael's chin deepened as he grinned. "Hey, that *would* be great, wouldn't it?"

"Well, you both know all the plays, don't you?" said Rick.

"Right." Michael sure did, having learned them all while helping Tom study and memorize them.

His eyes twinkled as Rick's words rolled over in his mind. In many ways Michael and Tom were a lot alike. Michael was born about six minutes later than Tom a little over twelve years ago. He was named after the grandfather on his mother's side, and Tom after the grandfather on his dad's side. It was the mutual wish of their mother and father that the boys be named that way.

Both boys had coal black hair, with tufts of it sticking up near the back of their heads. They both had brown eyes, wide eyebrows, and flat cheeks. The difference was the dimple in Michael's chin. Tom didn't have one. And then there was the sparkle in Michael's eyes, which seemed to be there constantly but which was only present in Tom's eyes when he had been complimented for something he'd done.

That was one thing Michael didn't understand about his brother. Tom had so much going for him, but sometimes he lacked confidence unless someone praised him. Michael couldn't figure out why Tom lacked confidence like that.

The game grabbed Michael's attention

again, and he tried to remain quiet this time as he watched the Eagles go into a huddle. A moment later they broke out of it, and Michael's heart began to pound as he tried to put himself in Tom's place.

If Rick only knew how much Tom and I work on this ESP thing, Michael thought, smiling to himself. *If he only knew that we are even considering a step* beyond *ESP, he'd think we've gone crazy.* That next step was Thought-Energy Control, or TEC, which Ollie Pruitt, the old man who lived next door to the twins, believed in and had told them about. And Mr. Pruitt was no dummy, or crazy, either. He used to be a science professor before he retired, and was in complete control of his senses.

Michael heard Tom bark signals. The ball was on the Eagles' forty-three-yard line, and it was first down. The score was still 0–0 after five minutes into the first quarter.

The ball snapped from center. Michael saw Tom take it and fade back, knew Tom was looking for a receiver. The ends, Bob Riley and Stan Bates, were running down the field, Riley on the left side, Bates on the right, both covered by Colts men.

Suddenly Stan cut sharply to his left, freeing himself from his guard. At that instant Tom let go of a pass. The ball looked like a large brown egg as it traveled through the air, wobbling ever so slightly. For a moment it seemed as if Tom had thrown it too far ahead of Stan, and Michael stiffened in his chair as he watched, every fiber in his body stretched like a guitar string.

Then Stan's outstretched hands caught the ball and pulled it to his chest. Stan cut at a diagonal angle toward the end zone, Colts men bolting after him. He was on the Colts' forty-one when he was brought down. It was another first down.

"Again, Tom! Again!" Rick shouted.

"No!" Michael cried. "They'll be expecting a pass now! We've got to run it! A power sweep should fool 'em! Yes, a power sweep!"

The power sweep would call for the running backs to spring toward the left side of the line to protect the quarterback, who would be carrying the ball.

The play Tom called for was a through-tackle plunge, and Vince did the plunging, gaining three yards.

Then Jim Berry fumbled the ball on a handoff, and the Colts recovered it.

Quickly, Coach Frank Cotter shoved in four substitutes. Tom was one of the players coming out. He sprinted off the field with his head lowered, as if the fumble was his fault and he felt guilty about it.

"That's okay, Tom," Michael said to him, trying to keep his brother's spirits up. "You had the right idea keeping the ball on the ground."

But Tom, taking off his helmet as he sat down, said nothing.

The Colts got the ball back into their territory, and, on the Eagles' thirty-five, they tried a pass. Kirk Tyler, the Eagles' safety man, intercepted it and carried it to the twenty-nine.

Coach Cotter put Tom back into the quarterback spot. This time Tom called for a power sweep, and it worked for thirty-five yards. A line plunge went for two.

Michael watched, feeling his nerves tingle again as he played his own secret, private game of quarterbacking the Eagles from his wheelchair.

A flat pass, he thought, as the Eagles went into a huddle. *Fake a handoff to Jim, who scoots off to the left. Then shoot a pass to Angie as he runs to the right.*

The Eagles broke out of the huddle and

went into formation. Tom barked signals. The ball was snapped. Tom faked a handoff to Jim, turned and shot a pass to Angie. Angie swung around the end of the line and ran as if an army of ants were after him. Moments later he was over! A touchdown!

Michael bounced up and down in his wheelchair, banging its armrests happily with his fists. "All right, Tom! All right!" he shouted.

He slapped Rick on the shoulder. "You know, I think we have it, Rick."

Rick looked at him. "Have what?" he asked curiously.

"ESP. I was thinking of that same play, and Tom called it. That's ESP, isn't it?"

Rick shrugged. "Or just plain coincidence," he said.

A hand rested on Michael's arm, and he looked around at his mother, a tall, trim woman with straight auburn hair, which she kept cut to just below her ears. Because of a cool breeze, she was wearing her beige, three-quarter-length coat.

Michael had forgotten she was at the game. She had been sitting in the first row of seats in the bleachers behind him. She was standing beside him now, looking worriedly at him through her steel-rimmed glasses.

"Michael, the way you're bouncing, you'll be falling out of that chair," she warned him.

"No, I won't, Mom," he assured her. "I'm okay."

Then her eyes widened as she looked at his face. "Michael, you're sweating!"

He drew his arm across his forehead, felt the perspiration, wiped it off, and smiled. "Of course, Mom. It's been an exciting game," he told her.

She tucked the blanket comfortingly

around his legs. "I don't want you to catch a cold," she said.

Just like a mother, Michael thought. "Oh, Mom, let me alone," he said, embarrassed. "I'm fine. Really I am."

Vince booted the ball between the up-rights for the extra point. 7–0, Eagles.

In the second quarter Angie latched onto a pass that put the ball on the Colts' eleven-yard line. After that it was easy riding for another score, Jim getting it with a plunge through left tackle from the two-yard line. Then Vince collected his second point after. 14–0, Eagles.

Four minutes before the half ended, the Colts' quarterback, Larry Tubbs, pulled one out of the hat. He took the snap from center, faked a handoff to his fullback, Jay Henderson, then rolled to the right and released a long pass to his left end, Pat June. Pat caught the pass and had clear sailing ahead of him as he went for the Colts' first touchdown. Larry's point-after kick was perfect. 14–7, Eagles.

There were two minutes to go before the half ended. Then one minute . . .

The Eagles were on the march, heading for another touchdown. The ball was on the Colts' eight-yard line. Tom was calling signals.

Michael sat stiffly in his chair, his hands gripping the armrests. His pulse throbbed. He saw the snap from center, and could almost feel the ball slide into his hands.

Grip the ball. Spread the fingers. Hand the ball off to Vince. Go, Vince, go!

Vince plowed through for three yards.

Quickly, the Eagles went into a huddle, scrambled out of it, ran again. It was another short gain.

The seconds ticked away. "Pass it!" Michael yelled, excitedly. "Pass it, Tom!"

Tom passed it, a bullet throw to Jim Berry, just left of the goalposts. Jim caught it.

"Way to go, Tom!" Michael cried, bouncing up and down in the chair, both fists raised in triumph. "You pulled it off!"

Rick glanced around at him. "Hey, man. You called it again."

Michael's face wreathed with a smile. "Sure. We've got ESP, I tell you."

Vince's kick for the point after was off to the side. But the lead was safe, 20–7.

Seconds later the horn blared, ending the first half.

Rick and the other guys on the bench dashed off to join their team for a meeting with the coach in the west end zone. The Colts were running to join their coach, in the east end zone.

Michael sat back, took a deep breath, and relaxed.

"Can I get you a hot dog and a soda?" his mother asked him. She had come up in front of him, her warm voice like a song in the cool September air. The breeze played with the straight ends of her hair.

"That'd be great, Mom," he said. "I'm starved."

He wasn't really, but a hot dog and a soda would taste good right now.

"I'll be right back," she said, and hurried away.

Michael's father came up beside him. "Enjoying the game, son?" he asked. Mr. Curtis was six feet tall, slim and pencil-straight. The back of his left hand was scarred from a burn he had received while fighting a barn fire three years ago. He was a volunteer fireman with the Bruner Volunteer Fire Company.

"I sure am, Dad," Michael replied.

"Tom's doing all right, isn't he?"

"He's doing real well." Michael paused, thinking. *I won't say anything to him about ESP. He might not believe in it.*

"Got something on your mind?" his father asked. His brown eyes bored gently into Michael's. Crescent lines formed around his mouth as he smiled.

Michael looked at him, surprised. "No. Why should I?"

"I thought for a minute you wanted to say something else."

Michael frowned, then nodded. "I did, Dad. But maybe you'll laugh at me if I say it."

Mr. Curtis shrugged. "Okay. I promise I won't laugh."

Michael hesitated, then looked closely at his father. "Do you believe in ESP, Dad?"

His father looked at him, straightened up

to his full height, and ran a hand across his chin. "Well, I do, to some extent, Michael. Why?"

"Maybe you think I'm crazy, but it seemed as if every time I called a play in my mind, Tom would call it. Isn't that ESP?"

His father smiled and lifted his slender shoulders in a shrug. "Well, it could be ESP," he said. "Maybe you and Tom have a thing going between you."

"Yeah," said Michael, and looked away. No use pursuing the subject any further. He could tell his father wasn't all that interested in whatever Michael wanted to say. He was just being polite.

Michael was glad when his mother came with his hot dog and soda.

The second half of the game went by as painlessly for the Eagles as the first half had. Vince scored on a twenty-six-yard run, and

Stan, on a pass. The Colts scored once, on an interception. It was Tom's poorest throw of the game. The Eagles won, 33–14, having missed a point-after attempt.

Mr. Curtis helped Michael into the backseat of the car, while Tom folded up the wheelchair and stuck it into the trunk. On the way home Mr. and Mrs. Curtis rehashed the game, throwing praises at practically every member of the Eagles team, including the tackles and guards, those unsung heroes few people ever think about. Meanwhile Tom kept shaking his head and condemning himself for throwing that stupid pass behind Bob Riley, the pass that was intercepted and resulted in the Colts' second touchdown.

"What're you kicking yourself for?" Mr. Curtis said to him. "It didn't hurt the game. You won, didn't you?"

The brothers looked at each other, and smiled.

"Guess I'm dumb, aren't I?" said Tom.

"No. I know how you feel, Tom," said Michael. "I think I'd feel the same way. I'm sure of it. *Exactly* the same way."

"Tell him what you told me about your ESP, Michael," said Mr. Curtis, a sly grin on his lips.

Tom looked at his brother. "What about it?"

Michael shrugged. "Oh, it's nothing."

"No. Tell me. I want to hear it."

"Okay, but later," said Michael. He didn't want to start talking about it again in front of his father. The next time it would be just for Tom's ears to hear.

It wasn't till after half past four, and the brothers were in Michael's room, that Michael explained about his ESP experience — or whatever it was — to Tom.

"It started off in the first quarter with that T-forty-three play," said Michael. "I called the play out loud, then kept wishing in my mind that you would call it. Did you hear me?"

Tom frowned. "When you called it out loud? No. But —" Suddenly he paused and looked hard into Michael's eyes.

"But, what?" asked Michael, his eyebrows arched.

"I'm not sure. I felt funny, that's all I know. Real funny. Weird is a better word, I guess."

"Weird? Why weird? What do you mean?"

"I don't know what I mean. I just can't explain it," said Tom.

"Was it almost as if somebody else was playing in your place? Was that how it felt?"

Tom stared at him. Tiny beads of sweat began to form on his forehead. "Something like that."

"Then you must've been thinking the same thing I was."

Tom looked at him curiously. "I was thinking about you, Mike. During a lot of that game I was thinking about you."

"And I was thinking about you," Michael admitted.

Tom got up and started pacing the floor slowly. He didn't say a word for several seconds. He was deep in thought.

"What are you thinking about, Tom?" his brother asked.

"About you and me — switching places. It's supposed to be impossible, I know. But —" Tom paused, and Michael felt goose bumps pop out on his arms. "Ever since that accident two years ago, you've spent most of your time in that wheelchair. You'll never play football again, or baseball, or track, or anything else that I enjoy doing."

"Heck, have I ever complained?" asked Michael.

The boys were ten when the accident had happened. A car had backed out of a driveway and had struck Michael while he was riding his bike on the sidewalk. Ever since then he hadn't been able to use his legs, and the doctor said he might never again.

"No," Tom said. "You've been super about that. It's great you can swim, and you've beaten me a dozen times at Ping-Pong. But I know how much you'd like to play other sports. Football, for example."

Michael nodded. "I'd give anything." Then he laughed. "Hey, I've already given my legs! Maybe they were the wrong things to give!" He made a face. "A stupid thing to say, wasn't it?"

Tom shook his head. "You have an attitude I can't believe, Mike."

"Heck, you're trying to say I'm bad off. I'm not. Legs aren't everything. I just can't walk or run, that's all." He was quiet for a moment, then looked his brother in the eye. "Still, I do miss playing football sometimes.

So tell me: Have you been thinking the same thing I've been thinking? About Ollie Pruitt's theory on TEC? Thought-Energy Control?"

"Yes! Let's talk with Ollie about it, okay? If anybody knows anything about it, it's Ollie."

"Right."

Michael's face brightened. "I bet we *can* do TEC, Tom. Wouldn't that be great?"

Tom smiled. "You bet it would. Come on. Let's go over and see him right now."

Excited about the prospect, Michael started toward the door ahead of Tom. Suddenly he stopped, and looked around at his twin brother.

"What now?" Tom asked, curious.

Michael smiled. "Tom, you're the greatest," he said. "I'm sure glad you're my brother." Then he turned and continued toward the door.

Ollie Pruitt lived in the tall, two-story house next door. It was set farther back from the street than any other house, was painted a butterscotch color, and was the only one with a steep, wood-shingled roof. His front and back lawns were covered with plants and flowers, one of his two favorite hobbies.

His other hobby was nobody else's business, except a handful of friends who were interested in the same thing. Those included the kids next door, Michael and Tom, who figured that Ollie kept the hobby a secret from most people because it was pretty far out. Some people might think that Ollie had gone loony if they knew — a good enough reason, the boys thought, why the old guy didn't want to share his secret with everybody.

He was watering a plant when the boys got to his place. They greeted each other. Ollie asked them about the outcome of the game, which channeled the conversation away from the boys' more important topic for a few minutes.

Then Ollie seemed to sense that the boys had not come to talk football; he lifted his faded brown hat, scratched his bald head, and looked at them with narrowed eyes.

"Well, what's on your collective mind?" he asked. "I can tell it ain't football."

The boys grinned.

"We'd like to talk with you about something, Mr. Pruitt," said Michael.

Michael was nervous, and he suddenly

wondered if he and Tom were doing the right thing.

Ollie Pruitt's eyes shifted from one brother to the other. "Something personal?"

"Yes."

"Okay. Come into my inner sanctum."

The boys followed him into the house, slowly, because Ollie — being somewhere between seventy and ninety years old — never rushed into doing anything. His wife had died long ago. He had no children, just a brother and a sister, neither of whom he had seen in forty years. They were probably both dead for all he knew, he had told the boys once.

His inner sanctum was a large room, lined with shelves of books, in the back of the house. Over a fireplace was the head of a ten-point deer. The carpet was worn clear through to the matting in some places, and the chairs looked like relics from George

Washington's day. All four corners of the redwood ceiling were laced with cobwebs. This was the fifth or sixth time the boys had visited him in here, and the room didn't look a bit different.

"Can I get you a drink?" Ollie asked. "Orange juice or something?"

"No, thanks," Michael said.

"Me neither," said Tom.

They looked at each other, each waiting for the other to break the barrier. Suddenly the tall grandfather clock next to the fireplace bonged, jolting Michael like an electric shock. The clock bonged four more times.

Ollie chuckled. "That's five o'clock. That racket should jar you boys into speaking your piece. No need to be shy about it. We understand each other, don't we? It's almost as if we have the same mind at times. Right?"

"Right," said Michael. He took a deep breath and went on. "Mr. Pruitt, Tom and I are sure we had an ESP experience today at the football game. I got to thinking of plays I thought he should call, and that's exactly what he did. He called them."

"I'm not surprised to hear that," said Ollie calmly. He sat down on a worn cushioned chair and motioned Tom to sit on the one next to him. "You boys are unique in that you think so much alike. ESP isn't all that strange, as you know."

"Well, it isn't only *that* we were thinking about, Mr. Pruitt," said Tom, darting a glance at his brother.

Ollie's eyes shifted from one boy to the other. "That so? What else have you got on your collective mind?"

Again the brothers looked at each other, neither of them quite sure whether to bring the subject up. Then Michael thought,

We've gone this far. We might as well go all the way. If Ollie thinks we've lost our marbles, we'll just go home and forget the whole thing.

"Mr. Pruitt," he said seriously, "you once told us that we were all just made up of particles of matter. You said that the day would come when a human being could transport himself to wherever he wished. Remember that?"

Ollie nodded. "That's right. As a matter of fact, some people believe that aliens on other planets are doing that very same thing this very minute."

"I've read about that, too," said Michael. "But remember when you told us that you're sure that two people — if they concentrated hard enough on it, and wished hard enough on it — could . . . well . . . could change places with each other?"

"Of course, I remember that," said Ollie,

his eyes brightening with interest. "By deep concentration, and wishing, you put your combined thought-energies to work through TEC, Thought-Energy Control. Your thought-energies project your mind out of your body and it goes where you want it to go. Michael would slip into Tom's clothes and Tom, into Michael's."

His eyes sparkled as he continued with his explanation of the phenomenon. "For instance, if you two concentrate your thought-energies as hard as you can, Tom would end up sitting in the wheelchair, and you, Michael, would become the healthy athlete."

The boys' eyes glowed with enthusiasm over the idea of experimenting with this wonderful phenomenon.

Mr. Pruitt smiled. "But, remember, it will take *extra* energy. *Extra* concentration. *Extra* wishing. Chances are that you two might not make it on the first try, or even the second or third. But you mustn't give up. That's the secret. It will happen. It might take a lot out of you in the beginning, but it will happen if you stick with it. And after you've done it once, it'll come easier."

A proud grin spread across his wrinkled face. "Is that what you've got on your minds? You'd like to try TEC?"

Michael's heart pounded. He looked at Tom. Tom's face was beaming.

"Yes, we'd like to try it," Michael said excitedly. "Before the accident that paralyzed my legs, I did nearly all the things that Tom does. Played football, baseball, ran in track —"

"He ran faster than I did," Tom cut in. "And he was a better quarterback, too."

"There were a lot of things I did that he does," Michael went on. "We thought that if we tried TEC, then I'd have a chance to play again."

"A splendid idea," Ollie agreed enthusiastically. "I admire you. Both of you. Shows the love you have for each other. Okay, when and where would you like to try out TEC for the physical exchange?"

"At the football games," said Tom.

Ollie nodded. "Good." His eyes narrowed again. "Just remember, it's concentration and wishing — extraordinary concentration, extraordinary wishing — that will get your thought-energies working. And you'll do it. I'm sure you will."

"Thanks, Mr. Pruitt," said Tom. He got up from his chair. "We're sure glad you're our neighbor, Mr. Pruitt," he added.

Ollie took off his hat and set it on the floor. His bald head was pink, and wrinkled in back. "You boys give me a lot of pleasure, too," he admitted. "It was a good many years, you know, that I lived like a hermit in this house, just because people figured I was a little touched upstairs." He ran a finger in small circles around his right ear. "Then you boys came along. These past five years have been the happiest since before my wife passed away. Yes, sir — books are all right, but they just can't take the place of people."

"Thanks, Mr. Pruitt," said Michael. "Well, we'll be seeing you."

"Right. And I'll see you," said Ollie, "at the games."

On Monday, after school, Michael sat on the sidelines, watching the Eagles work out on the east end of the football field. The Moths were working out on the west end at the same time.

He was among a couple of dozen kids. Some he knew, some he didn't. Some of them were girls. Two of them, Sally Barton and Martha Withers, were doing a lot of talking and giggling. They just came to hang around the guys, anyway. Neither one had a boyfriend, and the way they talked and giggled it wasn't hard to understand why they didn't.

Some of the other girls, Michael thought, weren't bad. Vickie Marsh, for example. She was pretty skinny, but she had beautiful skin and long blond hair. She had brains, too. Tom talked about her once in a while, sometimes sounding as if he liked her just a little. But Tom wasn't stuck on her. He had said so.

The backfield men drilled on running patterns, the linemen on blocking. Then the two quarterbacks, Tom and Kirk, took turns throwing passes to the ends. Michael watched Tom's every move with avid concentration. He began to think more and more of himself in Tom's place; he was concentrating so hard that he could almost feel the smoothness of the leather in his hands as the center snapped the football. He tried to think of himself in Tom's place as Tom faked a handoff, faded back, came to a standstill, and drilled a pass to an end.

There was more to passing than just throwing the ball, whether the pass was short or long. The important thing was to throw it ahead of the receiver; and you had to time it right or you were in trouble. Michael knew that. He had studied all the aspects of quarterbacking a team by watching television, by reading books, and by watching Tom.

After the initial drills were over, Coach Cotter had the team split up into squads. Because there were only eighteen players, the coach had the eleven regulars work on running plays against a seven-man defensive line. On pass plays he boosted the defense to eleven men to make it tougher for the passers and receivers. Nevertheless, Tom was able to complete four passes out of five.

Kirk completed two out of five. But this was only his first year as a quarterback. Michael figured that in another year he'd be as good as — or maybe better than — Tom.

When the drills were over, some of the players dropped on the grass and lay on it as if they couldn't move another step. Lumpy Harris, a lineman, was one of them. There was almost enough of him to make two linemen.

Stogey Snyder was another. He wasn't quite as fat as Lumpy, but if he were to race with a turtle, chances were that he'd come in second.

Some of the guys stopped and talked with the girls, and Michael glanced at Vickie Marsh. He wasn't surprised to see that she was standing there all alone. The girls who had been with her had left her stranded while they went to meet their heroes. But her eyes were on somebody, and Michael saw that she was looking at Tom.

Then, as Tom was coming toward Michael, Tom glanced in her direction, and a faint smile came over his lips.

"Hi, Vickie," he greeted her.

"Hi, Tom," she said.

Then she looked at Michael and their eyes met squarely. "Hi, Michael!" she exclaimed. "How are you?"

"Fine, thanks," he said.

She came toward them. A soft breeze blew a strand of her hair across her face and she pushed it back. "Who are you playing on Saturday?" she asked Tom.

He thought a moment, then glanced at Michael. It was obvious he couldn't remember, and Michael wondered if Vickie's presence fogged up his memory.

"I think the Moths," said Tom, unsure.

"The Scorpions," Michael corrected him, and grinned. "We play the Moths the Saturday after."

"Oh, that's right." Tom blushed. Just then he seemed to have discovered a smudge of dirt on his helmet and started to rub it off.

"The Scorpions?" Vickie echoed. "Wow! Are they good?"

Tom shrugged. "I don't know. We'll find out when we play them."

He stopped rubbing at the smudge, looked up and beyond her. "Your friends are waiting for you," he said.

She turned and looked behind her. "They're not my friends," she said abruptly. "Well, not all of them." She swung her head back to let the wind blow the hair away from her face. "I'd better go, though. See you around."

"Okay," said Tom.

She turned and ran off, her hair flaring out like the wings of a butterfly.

"I think she has a crush on you, brother," Michael said, as they started off the field.

"You're crazy," said Tom.

"And I bet you like her, too."

"What makes you think that?"

"You forgot who we play this Saturday, that's what. And I know your memory isn't that bad."

Tom laughed. "Yeah. Guess that was stupid, wasn't it?"

They reached the gate and got on the sidewalk.

"Did you concentrate on what I was doing?" Tom asked, changing the subject. "Because I was concentrating, almost every minute."

"I did. But nothing happened. Maybe we're just not concentrating and wishing hard enough."

"And maybe it's a lot of baloney," said Tom. He sounded defeated. "Maybe it's just impossible to do what we're thinking of doing."

Michael looked at him. His eyes were narrowed and intensely serious.

"But you heard Ollie, Tom. He said it is possible. And I think it is, too. We both have to concentrate very, very hard on it. You do want to do it, don't you? You're not changing your mind?"

"Of course I want to do it. If it's possible, I want to do it very much. It would be the greatest thing in the world that has ever happened to me."

"And it will happen, because I'm sure we can do it, Tom." Mike's eyes gleamed with confidence. "We've just got to concentrate and wish on it with all our might, that's all."

The Eagles practiced every night of the week except on Friday, and each night Vickie Marsh was present at the field, too.

On Thursday she was there with just one girl, whom she introduced to Michael and Tom as her friend Carol Patterson. Carol, dark-haired and not quite as skinny as Vickie, hardly said a word all the time they were together. She had been too busy eating a Popsicle.

"Man, that Carol is some creep," said Michael, on their way home Thursday evening. "Can't she talk?"

"She said 'Hello,'" replied Tom.

"I know. But that's all she said."

"Maybe it's a good thing," Tom said. "How would you have liked it if she had kept jabbering every minute?"

"It would have driven me up a wall."

"Right."

The game on Saturday started at the usual time, 2 P.M. It was a warm day. Clouds hovered in the sky like balls of cotton, hardly moving. The grandstand, speckled with both Eagles and Scorpions fans, buzzed like a beehive.

Michael, in his wheelchair, was at his usual place just left of the players' bench. He had not asked for the privilege of watching the games from this vantage spot. Coach Cotter had granted it to him, a privilege Michael sincerely appreciated.

He remembered that Ollie Pruitt had said

he'd see them at the games. He looked over his right shoulder, and then over his left.

Suddenly, Michael's hand rose and waved, and he shouted, "Mr. Pruitt!"

The old man was sitting in the second row near the end of the bleachers, his hat pulled down to shield his eyes from the sun.

"Hi, Michael!" he answered. "Good luck, boy!"

A couple of kids in front of Ollie Pruitt turned and looked up at him. And he smiled back at them.

Good old Mr. Pruitt, thought Michael. *Maybe with him close by, Tom and I will have luck in doing what we want to do.*

The Scorpions won the toss and chose to receive. The teams lined up. Vince Forelli kicked off. The boot was a poor one, slicing off toward the right side of the field. A Scorpion caught it and carried it to his own forty-two-yard line, where Butch Bogger smeared him.

The Scorpions got into a huddle. Seconds later they broke out of it and ran to the line of scrimmage. Terry Fisher, their quarterback, began barking signals.

Playing in the linebacker positions for the Eagles were Vince, Jim, and Angie. Tom was in the safety slot.

The center snapped the ball. Terry got it, turned, handed it off to fullback Ted Connors. Ted bucked through right tackle for a gain of four yards.

On the next play Nibbs McCay, the Scorpions' right halfback, took a handoff and sped around left end. He got good blocking, then stiff-armed Rick Howell for a gain of four yards before Rick regained his balance, cycloned after him, and pulled him down with a flying tackle.

A short pass over the right side of the line gave the Scorpions a first down. They were in Eagle territory now and hopping with total confidence.

Michael looked at Tom and began to think of playing in Tom's place. He didn't know for certain whether intense, deep concentration and wishing — both on his part and on Tom's — would really induce their thought-energies to let them exchange places, but then again, maybe Ollie Pruitt was right and switching places with another person whose interests and thoughts were attuned to your own was entirely possible if you concentrated hard enough.

So Michael began focusing his thoughts; he watched Tom's every move while he pictured himself making the moves. Only Tom, playing safety, wasn't doing much on defense. He was just making sure no Scorpion got past him.

The Scorpions had the ball on the Eagles' thirty-four-yard line when Doug Morton was called on a clipping charge, a fifteen-yard penalty. The ball was spotted on the nineteen, and it indeed looked as if there would be no stopping the Scorpions.

Ted Connors bucked for a three-yard gain, then again for five yards.

Michael could almost sense what was being said in the Eagles' huddle as they tried to anticipate what the Scorpions would do next.

"Watch for a pass! Get Terry, you linebackers! Try to stop him!"

The Eagles scrambled to their defensive positions, Tom in the end zone, his legs spread slightly apart, his arms bent at the elbows. Again, Michael tried to picture himself in Tom's place, standing there as Tom was standing, feeling the electric excitement.

Terry shouted signals. The ball was centered. He got it, faded back. Helmets crashed against helmets, shoulder pads against shoulder pads. And then there were black-and-red uniforms dotting the end zone, which was also sprinkled with the white-and-maroon uniforms of the Eagles.

Michael felt his heart pound as he saw Terry throw the ball in a perfect spiral toward the right side of the end zone. A Scorpion was sprinting for the corner, an Eagle after him. The Eagle was number 80, Bob Riley.

"Get it, Bob!" Michael shouted. "Get it!"

Bob didn't get it. But the Scorpion did. It was a touchdown.

Ted Connors kicked for the point after, and it was good. Scorpions 7, Eagles 0.

Michael felt a sinking in his breast, just as Tom must have felt. Getting behind by seven points so soon would drain a pound of energy out of anybody.

Ted Connors kicked off for the Scorpions. The kick was long, shallow, and straight as a string. Tom caught it and bolted up the field, dodging a couple of Scorpions and taking advantage of good blocking by Don Cleaver and Stan Bates. Tom was fast and agile, an excellent broken-field runner. As Tom spun this way and that to avoid would-be tacklers, Michael again pictured himself in Tom's place. As fast as Tom was, Michael knew that he was even faster. That he *had been* faster before the accident. If he could be in Tom's place now —

He concentrated and wished hard on the exchange, forgetting that he was in a wheel-chair as he tried to tune in on Tom's thoughts, and Tom's moves.

He hardly noticed it when he began to

sweat. The Eagles had the ball on their forty-six-yard line, and Tom was calling signals. The ball was snapped. Tom took it, faded back, looked for a receiver, and then heaved a long pass down the left side of the field. Tom watched the soaring ball; Michael watched it. Michael's heart pounded. He hoped that the throw wasn't too far out of reach of Bob Riley, the intended receiver.

The ball sailed like a gliding bird. It came down at the end of its arc and dropped into Bob's outstretched hands. Michael thought his heart was going to stop as the ball slipped out of Bob's hands, bounced up, flipped a couple of times, and then was drawn back again into the security of Bob's arms.

"Good go, Bob!" Michael yelled. "Now, run, man! Run!"

He was pounding his fist in the air as he watched Bob sprint down the field, a Scorpion on his tail. But Bob, a long-legged kid who was as fast as they came, kept widening the gap between himself and the would-be tackler.

And then Bob was in the end zone, slowing down as he circled around the goalposts, the ball raised high over his head. It was a touchdown! The Eagles' fans roared and cheered. Some whistled.

Michael raised his fists in triumph. "Way to go, guys!" he shouted.

Vince kicked for the extra point. It just cleared the bar. 7–7.

The teams lined up again for the kickoff. Vince kicked. Ted Connors caught the end-over-end liner, ran up to the Scorpions' thirty-four-yard line, and was tackled.

Terry Fisher called signals, took the snap, handed it off to Nibbs McCay. Nibbs blasted through right tackle for five yards.

On the next play, Lumpy Harris moved

before the ball was in play. It was a five-yard penalty.

Great, Michael thought, socking the armrests of his wheelchair in disgust. A first down for the Scorpions.

He suddenly thought of Ollie Pruitt, and glanced back to look at him. He was startled as he saw Ollie looking directly at him, as if Ollie knew that he, Michael, was going to turn and look at him at that same instant.

Ollie's lips moved. "Have faith," they seemed to say.

Michael nodded, and looked away.

The ball was spotted on the Scorpions' forty-four-yard line. In three plays they got it to the Eagles' twenty-eight.

First down and ten.

The Scorpions were moving, and they seemed to be unstoppable.

Terry called signals. Michael, watching intently, anticipated a running play. It wasn't called. Terry got the snap and dropped back, looking for a receiver.

Michael saw him first. It was Eddie Stone — Stoney — running down the right side of the field. There appeared to be no one near him.

Get him, Tom! Get him! Michael screamed to himself.

His body pulsed, aching to move. Every fiber in his arms and legs quivered as they struggled to react.

And then something strange happened. *He was running down the field! He was running after Stoney! He was in Tom's shoes, in Tom's uniform!*

The Thought-Energy Control had worked! He had exchanged places with Tom!

Just short of the ten-yard line, Michael lunged at Stoney, caught him by the waist, and brought him down.

"Nice tackle, Tom," said Angie, as Michael got to his feet.

Now came another tough ordeal. How to avoid being recognized? If the guys looked at and listened to him closely enough, could they see he wasn't Tom, even though they were twins?

Other than the dimple in Michael's chin, the brothers looked alike. They had the same color eyes and hair. They even parted their hair on the same side. Was that enough to protect his identity? Michael wondered. He just had to wait and see — and keep his fingers crossed.

He trotted back into the end zone and waited for the next play.

The Scorpions tried an end-around run, and lost a yard. Then Terry faked a handoff to Ted Connors, faded back a few feet, and shot a pass to Buzz Haner.

Michael, seeing the play forming, started toward Buzz even before Terry had released the ball. The bullet pass was on the money, except that Michael got there first. He caught the ball, pulled it into his arms, and started down the field. His legs churning with power, he sprinted across the five-yard line . . . the ten . . . the fifteen . . . the twenty . . .

Not a Scorpion got near him. He went all the way.

As he crossed the goal line and lifted the ball high over his head, he cried out in his mind to Tom: *Let's change places, Tom! I'm tired!*

It happened quickly. In the next instant he was back in his wheelchair, looking out upon the field, watching the guys showering Tom with praises for making that interception and sprinting all the way down the field for a touchdown!

Michael grinned happily, not minding at all that Tom was receiving the accolades. He turned, caught Ollie's eye, and gave him the "V for victory" sign. Ollie acknowledged it by showing Michael the same sign, plus his big, teeth-revealing smile.

Michael turned his attention back to the game, the resounding din of the applause slowly diminishing. Scoring, he thought, was of secondary importance. What was more important was that their thought-energies had worked. By concentrating and wishing as hard as they could, they had accomplished the miracle of exchanging places. That, at last, he had gotten to play football again!

He closed his eyes and leaned his head back, not even interested in seeing Vince kick for the extra point. A loud groan told him that the kick wasn't good, anyway. So the score remained: Eagles 13, Scorpions 7.

The Eagles had a rough second quarter. Twice they were penalized for being offside, and twice they were hit with fifteen-yard penalties — for clipping and for holding — a total loss of forty yards, while the Scorpions chalked up another touchdown.

Each team scored once during the second half, but it was the Scorpions who pulled the squeaker, 21–20.

"What's the matter?" Tom asked Michael

when they were alone for a brief moment after the game. "Didn't you want to go back in?"

"No. I was too tired," said Michael. "And nervous. I was afraid I might ruin it."

"Ruin the game? Heck, we lost it, anyway."

"Yeah, I know. But I was bushed. Scared, too."

"Scared? Of what?"

"That somebody might sense that something was different. That would've ruined it. Did you see Ollie?" He looked over his shoulder as he spoke. He saw Ollie and waved. Ollie grinned and waved back.

"Yes, I saw him." Tom smiled. "Maybe his being here helped."

"Uh-oh, squash it," said Michael, lowering his voice. "Here come Vickie and Carol."

The girls came toward them, grinning like

Cheshire cats. Carol was eating a Popsicle again.

"Hi," greeted Vickie. "Sorry you lost."

Tom shrugged. "That second quarter beat us," he said.

Carol looked at Michael. "I guess you really get hung up in a game, don't you?" she said. "I don't know how many times I said 'Hi' to you, and you never turned around once."

Michael stared at her through widened eyes. "I'm sorry. What quarter was that?"

The girls looked at each other to verify the exact time.

"The first quarter, wasn't it?" said Carol, frowning.

Vickie nodded. "Right. The first quarter."

The first quarter, thought Michael. *It was probably when Tom and I had exchanged places. Oh, great. That's just great.*

He grinned nervously at her. "That's right. I really do get hung up in a game. I'm sorry, Carol. I'm really sorry."

"Oh, that's okay," she said. "I wouldn't get mad at you for a little thing like that."

Michael was glad when his mother and father arrived to break up the party. Tom introduced the girls to them, then the girls left, and the Curtis family went on its way home. They rehashed some of the plays of the game, while Michael restrained himself from telling them about the complete, wonderful success of their thought-energy process. He wouldn't ever tell, no matter what. That was one thing that was a bound secret between him and Tom. And, of course, Ollie Pruitt.

They weren't home more than half an hour, just long enough for Tom to get out of his uniform and into clean clothes and knock off a sandwich, when Tom suggested to Michael that they go next door to see Ollie. The idea had been bubbling inside of Michael's head, too.

"Sure!" he said excitedly.

They found Ollie cutting the shoots of a sea grape plant.

"Well, howdy, boys," he greeted them cheerfully. "Good game. Too bad you lost it." He held the shoots while his eyes flicked from one brother to the other. "It worked, didn't it? You got your TEC to work perfectly."

"Yes, we did, Mr. Pruitt," Michael exclaimed. His body quivered with joy and excitement. At least they could share their experience with Ollie. He was a true believer. He would appreciate it.

Michael explained it to Ollie first, how he had felt when the game had started, how he had tried to concentrate and wish so hard to put himself in Tom's place; and then Tom butted in, saying how he had concentrated on the switch, too. And, suddenly, in one split second, the *actual* exchange: Tom in the wheelchair in Michael's clothes, and Michael on the field in Tom's uniform.

"We proved it's possible, Mr. Pruitt!" Michael said proudly. "And we're going to do it again!"

Ollie's eyes sparkled. "Of course you're going to do it again. You've got a good thing going, not only for you, Michael, but for Tom, too. Now he can rest while you play, and nobody will know the difference!"

7

Eight and two.

The ball was on the Eagles' twenty-two-yard line. It was the following Saturday. They were playing the Moths. The Eagles huddled, split, trotted to the line of scrimmage.

"Eight! Nine! Eleven! Hip! Hip! Hip!"

Jack centered the ball. Tom caught it, stepped back, faked a handoff to Jim. Jim bolted through the line, pulling a guard and a linebacker after him as if they were magnetized.

On the right side of the field, Angie was

running like a gazelle. Hans Steiner, the Moths' left end, was after him.

On the left side of the field was a stampede. Right end Chuck Willis and linebacker Moonie Jones were pounding the turf after Bob Riley.

Lumpy was doing a good job blocking his man, Moe Finney, the Moths' lanky guard. Moe might as well have been trying to push aside an army tank.

But Nick Podopolis got through. Nick was the Moths' middle linebacker on defense and played fullback on offense. He was big, fast, and strong. He was a midget bull.

Michael saw him bust through the line between Jack Benson and Doug Morton. Nick went after Tom with his short, chunky legs churning like pistons. His broad shoulders were down, and his arms were stretched out like tentacles.

Michael felt his heart rise to his throat. He

glanced over the field and saw that Angie had buttonhooked in, clearing himself from Hans. Then he glanced back at Tom. An electric shiver coursed through him as he saw that Nick had Tom on the run. Tom was being chased back toward his own goal line!

Concentrating hard, hoping that his thought-energies would work, Michael tried to switch places with Tom. This was the second quarter and Tom looked tired. That long, sixty-two-yard touchdown run in the first quarter must have drained some of the strength out of him.

But Michael knew that if Tom wasn't concentrating and wishing, too, exchanging places with him was out of the question. And apparently Tom wasn't, for the exchange never came about. Tom was smeared on his own three-yard line.

"Oh, too bad!" said a voice behind Michael. He recognized it immediately. It belonged to Carol Patterson. He had a notion to turn and look at her; he wondered whether she would be eating another Popsicle. But he didn't.

The loss of yardage put the Eagles where the Moths no doubt wanted them. Against the wall. On their second play the Eagles fumbled the ball. The Moths recovered it, then went over for the touchdown. It was Nick who scored, and Nick, again, who kicked the extra point. Eagles 7, Moths 7.

Michael sat in his wheelchair, hunched forward, as the teams lined up for the kickoff. He was anxious to go in, but was Tom as anxious to come out? he wondered. *Darn Tom!* he thought angrily. *Now that I can go in the game, he won't let me! He won't cooperate!*

Michael sat back, fuming. What a rotten deal to make. Tom had agreed to cooperate on the thought-energy control, but now that they made it work, he was reneging! What a brother!

Suddenly Michael stiffened in his chair. What was he doing? Why was he making such a terrible judgment of Tom just because their exchange had not been made now when he, Michael, wanted it?

Tom was too wrapped up in the game now. That was the reason, of course. The game was tight. And, being quarterback, Tom had to mastermind the moves. The coach had given him almost full rein to run the team. That *had* to be the reason Tom wasn't concentrating on TEC.

The smart thing to do, Michael figured, was for him and Tom to decide before a game when to concentrate on their thought-energies. It would save time, and be less frustrating, too.

He glanced over his shoulder at the seat where he had seen Ollie at the last game. This time Ollie's attention was on the game.

Michael smiled, and looked away.

He watched Moonie kick off. It was a nice, long, shallow boot. Tom gobbled it up on the fifteen and did some fancy broken-field running before he was brought down on the thirty-three. Michael smiled with admiration. *Darn it! But that kid can really run!* he thought.

Tom called pass plays on the first two downs. Neither one worked.

He glanced toward the sideline. He looked bushed. Was he worried, too? *Could be,* Michael thought.

Michael waved to him. Tom answered by barely making a gesture. Was he looking for help? Maybe even an exchange?

"The T-forty-three drive!" Michael said,

loudly enough to carry only ten feet. "The T-forty-three drive!"

The Eagles broke out of the huddle and hustled to the line of scrimmage. Michael watched Tom step up close to the center, the other three backfield men forming a T behind him.

Michael clapped with joy. They were going to run! It was the T-43 drive play!

Tom barked signals. As the words popped out of his mouth, Michael began to concentrate. He pictured himself in Tom's place, crouching as Tom was crouching, looking over the line as Tom was looking, yelling the signals as Tom was yelling.

Jack snapped the ball, faked a handoff to Vince, then chucked a short lateral pass to Jim. Driving forward like a small bulldozer, Jim plowed through tackle for twelve yards!

Michael saw Tom leap with joy, saw Tom

turn toward him, his fists held high as he whooped it up.

Michael lifted his arms, too, as he joined in with the cry. He felt a thrill, the exhilaration of the play's success.

Then, suddenly, he was on the field! He was in Tom's shoes, in Tom's uniform! He was in the game!

He looked toward the sideline. There sat Tom in the chair, except that Tom was dressed in Michael's clothes.

They got in a huddle. Michael put his hands on his knees as he glanced quickly at the faces around him. The fear still lurked that one of the players might sense something was different, but he had to risk it. He would cope with that problem when, and if, it came.

"Wild dog! On two!" said Michael, hoping that a pass play would surprise the Moths.

The Eagles broke out of the huddle, assembled at the line of scrimmage.

"Four! Seven! Hip! Hip! Hip!" Michael barked.

He took the snap, faded back, glanced first toward the right, then the left. The ends were doing a good job of blocking their men. And Vince looked free as he ran down toward the sideline, moving into Moth territory. He looked back and Michael whipped the pass to him, throwing the ball ahead of Vince so that he would catch it on the run.

The play worked for eight yards.

Another quick pass over the line of scrimmage netted four yards and a first down.

This time, as a change of pace, Michael called for a running play. But Angie fumbled the ball as Michael handed it off to him. The ball bounced back to the Eagles' forty-nine-yard line, where Michael pounced on it like a cat.

Second and eighteen.

"That was a lousy handoff, Tom," said Vince disgustedly.

Michael blushed. "Sorry, Vince."

"Why don't we try a long pass, Tom?" said Bob in the huddle.

"Yeah," agreed Stan. "Way out in the left flat. I can run the pants off that Steiner guy."

"Good idea," said Jim. "Give me the hand-off and I'll heave it out to him."

"Hold it," said Michael. "We're wasting time. They'll expect a pass. We have to try something different. A surprise. Seventeen sprint-out pass. If I can't work it, I'll run it."

Nobody contradicted him. They broke out of the huddle.

He called signals. The ball was snapped. Michael started to fade back, then ran to the right, parallel with the line of scrimmage, while he looked for his receiver, Stan Bates. Stan seemed to be free, so Michael started to lift the ball to his shoulders to attempt the pass.

Suddenly he saw a Moth sprinting hard toward Stan, and Michael knew that an attempted pass might be disastrous.

He pulled the ball against his side and ran. He ran as hard as he could, bolting around right end as Jim Berry threw a fine block on the Moth end.

Up the field, Stan blocked the Moth safety man, clearing the field for Michael, who went all the way.

A kick between the uprights put the Eagles in the lead, 14–7.

Vince slapped Michael happily on the back, then looked at him squarely in the eyes.

"Can you believe it?" he said, grinning.

"For a minute there, watching you run, I had a flash that it was Michael out here. Remember how fast he used to be? No one could catch him." Vince cocked his head to one side. "Guess you guys are more alike than I thought, huh?"

Michael's heart flip-flopped. His face turned red, and he grinned back to hide his embarrassment — and his fear that Vince might get more nosy.

"Nice kick, Vince," was all he said, and he trotted back across the field, with the rest of the guys, for the next kickoff.

The Moths were able to carry off only three plays, netting them enough yardage to get them to the Eagles' thirty-eight, when the first half ended.

As the team came walking tiredly off the field, Michael concentrated on his thought-energies again. He sensed that his thoughts and Tom's were in direct communication. In seconds he and Tom were back to their normal selves again.

Michael was very tired, almost to the point of exhaustion, but the experience had been fantastic. Imagine, he thought, he had gotten a touchdown. It was his second. He had scored the first one in the game against the Scorpions when he had intercepted a pass.

But this one he had done on his own. He had decided on the option play, and had made it work.

"Wasn't that run just fantastic?" a voice cried behind him.

He turned just as Carol burst around the left side of his wheelchair. He saw that she didn't have a Popsicle this time, and decided she was more normal than he had expected.

No person could afford — let alone eat — Popsicles all day long, he told himself.

"I've got to agree," he said. "It was."

He looked for Vickie, and saw her coming toward them unhurriedly, her eyes across the field, probably looking at Tom.

"Hi, Vickie," he said.

"Hi, Michael," she greeted him, flashing her warm smile. "How are you?"

"Fine. What do you think of that touchdown run Tom just made?"

"It was great."

"Yeah," he said, cracking a wry grin. "I thought so, too."

His grin broadened. If these girls only knew who had really made that touchdown, they'd die!

"Michael," said Carol, looking at him with her large eyes, "did you ever wish that you —" She hesitated, looked away, then looked at him again. "You wouldn't mind if I asked you a personal question, would you?"

He shrugged. "No. Go ahead, ask."

"Well —" She glanced down and started to burrow a toe into the hard surface of the earth near the front left wheel of his wheelchair. "Do you ever wish that you were able to play football? I mean — I know it's a stupid question because you . . . you can't . . . but I just wondered."

No one had ever asked him a question like that before. But he didn't mind. "I know what you mean," he said. "The answer is yes. I might as well be honest about it. I have wished that I could play. But it doesn't bother me very much that I can't." Oh, how he would like to tell her more!

She nodded, and shrugged. "Gee," she said.

"Gee, what?"

"Oh, nothing. Just gee." And she laughed.

The second half went well for the Moths. Jinx Roberts, their tall, scrambling quarterback, lapped up thirty yards on two runs, then heaved a touchdown pass to Hans Steiner that put the Moths one point behind the Eagles. Nick's kick for the extra point was off the mark by two yards, leaving the score: Eagles 14, Moths 13.

Then, just thirteen seconds before the third quarter was over, Tom fumbled a snap from center.

Michael almost pushed himself out of the chair as he tried to see who had recovered the ball. The action had stopped only a few yards away from the Eagles' goal line. If the Moths had recovered it, the game would be close to a loss for the Eagles.

Suddenly, the ref, standing over a player who was smothering the ball, jabbed a finger in the direction of the Eagles' goal line! And Moth players started to jump up and down jubilantly! It was the Moths' ball! They had recovered it!

Michael was sick. "Oh, no!" he groaned. "Oh, no! Tom, why did you have to fumble there?"

Nick Podopolis tried a line plunge and gained two yards.

"Hold 'em!" Michael shouted along with the hundreds of other Eagles fans. "Hold 'em, you guys!"

With four seconds to go before the quarter ended, Nick bucked the line again. This time he went over. His kick for the extra point was good, and the Moths went into the lead, 20–14.

The horn blew and the teams exchanged goals.

Tom caught Nick's long, spiraling kick, and brought it back to his own thirty-four. He looked bushed, Michael thought. Or perhaps he was depressed over the fumble he had made.

Michael began to concentrate on his thought-energies again, hoping that Tom would do likewise. This might be an excellent time for him and his brother to change places again.

But Michael failed to tune in on Tom's thought waves. Was Tom stubbornly refusing to concentrate on TEC because he wanted to make up for that fumble? Or was something else going on?

After a while, Michael, disgusted, gave up trying to make contact with Tom. *The heck with him,* he thought. *I'm not going to sit here and beg him to exchange places with me all the time. Anyway, maybe I'm wrong. Maybe I'm asking for too much. It's enough that Tom lets me play in his place once in a while.*

He sat there quietly and watched the Eagles take a battering from the Moths.

Suddenly, with five minutes left to play, Michael began to feel the vibrations that told him that Tom was trying to communicate with him! He looked at Tom, and joy welled up in him. He apologized silently to Tom for thinking that Tom had reneged on him, and concentrated as hard as he could on TEC.

The Eagles had the ball on their own forty-four-yard line. Michael thought he understood the problem. Tom had tried his best to get the ball moving toward the Moths' goal, but he just couldn't do it. And now he was asking for Michael's help.

In a moment the exchange was made. Michael was on the field, and Tom was in Michael's wheelchair.

Michael and the rest of the Eagles were in a huddle.

"Seventeen sprint-out pass," said Michael. "On two!"

He was nervous as he got behind Jack Benson and barked signals. The play had to work. It just had to.

"Eighteen! Twenty-one! Hip! Hip!"

He caught the snap, faded back a few steps, and glided to the right. All at once he saw Moonie Jones, the Moths' tank-sized linebacker, break through the line and come at him.

Panic swept through Michael as he searched the flats for a receiver. Then he saw Bob Riley cutting in from the left side-line, evading his guard for a few seconds. Those few seconds could be enough.

With Moonie only three steps away from him, Michael let go a pass. It barely missed Moonie's outstretched hands as it sailed in a neat spiral down the field. The throw looked as if it might be too far away from Bob, but the swift-footed end put on more speed, caught the ball, and sprinted toward the goal line.

Five yards away from it, he was caught by Eddie Myles, the Moths' safety man, and brought down.

"Beautiful pass, Mike!" shouted a voice from the sideline. "Beautiful!"

Michael stared across the field at Tom, who was waving his clasped hands over his head.

Someone poked him in the ribs. He looked around at Vince, who was grinning broadly at him.

"Hear that? Your brother seems so shook up he doesn't even know who he is! He called you Mike!"

Michael almost froze to the spot. He felt a shiver buzz through him. His mouth twitched as he tried to smile, hoping that he could say something that wouldn't get Vince curious.

"Oh, he . . . uh . . . he pretends he plays in my place sometimes," Michael said, rather stiffly. "After all, he's stuck in that wheelchair most of the time. He likes to get out of it once in a while — mentally, anyway. You know what I mean."

"Yeah. I guess I do. It must be pretty tough for him."

"Sometimes," said Michael.

"Hurry up, you guys," Butch piped up, "before the ref slaps a penalty on us for delaying the game."

Thanks, Butch, Michael thought, grateful for the interruption. Relief swept over him as he took his time going to the huddle. He got to thinking about having helped the team, and Tom, by successfully throwing a pass that put the Eagles within scoring distance. Now he would like to have Tom himself be in the game and score a touchdown, by a run or a pass.

He concentrated hard for the exchange, hoping that Tom was tuned in to his thoughts.

Then suddenly it happened. He was in his wheelchair, and Tom was on the field.

"Hey! You're not listening to me!" a voice cried near his elbow. "I asked you a question!"

Startled, Michael turned and saw Carol beside him, a half-eaten Popsicle clutched in her hand.

"I — I'm sorry," he said. "I had my mind on that play. Would you mind repeating the question, please?"

"No, since I have to in order to get an answer," she replied, and giggled. "Have you ever thought of what you'd like to do when you grow up? I mean, when you're an adult?"

Michael shrugged. "No. I haven't thought about it. I think I'm still pretty young to think about what I want to do when I'm an adult."

She wiped a little blob of Popsicle off her chin. "I think you're pretty smart, you know that?"

Michael blushed. "I wouldn't say so."

"I would. Want me to get you a Popsicle?"

"No, thanks. I'm not hungry."

"You sure?"

"Yes, I'm sure."

"Okay. See you later, Michael."

She left.

What a girl, Michael thought. *She isn't the mousy type we had judged her to be at first.*

All at once he heard a shout on the field and saw Eagles players jumping up and down and hugging each other. He knew that he had missed seeing the touchdown. Darn Carol, anyway, for yakking to him during that crucial moment!

Vince made the kick good for the point after. Eagles 21, Moths 20.

That was the score when the game ended.

Michael and Tom rode home with their mother and father. They discussed the game, and the brothers winked at each other when their father praised Tom for that long touchdown run in the second quarter, and for his perfectly thrown long pass in the last quarter that had put the Eagles in touchdown territory.

"You had me worried for a while," Mr. Curtis confessed. "You looked so tired I wasn't sure that you'd be able to finish the game."

"But you did," Mrs. Curtis chimed in enthusiastically. "You seemed to perk up just when you needed it!"

"Just in the nick of time. Right, Mom?" Michael said, nudging Tom in the ribs.

"Right!"

Tom chuckled, and Michael joined in with him.

"What's so funny?" their mother asked, looking curiously at them.

Tom shrugged. "Oh, nothing, Mom. We're just pleased that you and Dad enjoyed the game, that's all."

When their mother looked away, the boys smothered another laugh.

"I've got an apology to make to you, Mike," said Tom, his voice lowered so it would not carry to the front seat.

"Apology? What for?"

"I knew you wanted to make an exchange that one time when I called for the T-forty-three-drive play. But I wanted to do it. You know what I mean? I'm sorry."

Michael grinned. "Apology accepted," he said softly.

Later that day the twins visited Ollie Pruitt and told him of their successful thought-energy experience.

"Heck, I knew it would work again," said Ollie confidently, as he snipped dead stems off a hibiscus plant in his yard. "You two boys are perfect specimens. You're both smart as a whip, and you've got faith. You're unique for this thought-energy process. I've told you that before." He straightened up, grunting a little. "Hear these old bones? They snarl at me every time I move. Well, tell me about it. Has anybody gotten curious after you exchanged places?"

"I had a close shave," Michael said. He glanced at Tom. "Remember when you yelled at me just after I completed a pass to Bob Riley? You said, 'Beautiful pass, Mike! Beautiful!' Well, Vince heard you."

"I remember it all right," said Tom. "I could've crawled into a wormhole. Rick Howell was sitting on the bench next to me. Even he looked at me and wondered if I had gone off my rocker."

"What did you say to Vince?" Ollie asked, a smile tugging at the corners of his mouth. "You got out of it okay, I hope?"

"Oh, I think I did," Michael replied. "I said that he — meaning me in the wheel-chair — pretends he plays in my place sometimes — meaning Tom's place. I said that *he's* always stuck in that wheelchair and likes to get out of it once in a while."

Ollie's eyes twinkled. "And he swallowed your explanation?"

"The whole bit."

Ollie chuckled and scratched his nose. "Well, you didn't lie to him. Every word you told him was true. You've just got to be careful, though, that you both remember who you are at all times. One big goof and you both might become so disturbed about it that you won't be able to do it again."

"Boy, that's right," said Tom, shooting a glance at Michael. "I hadn't thought about that."

Michael shook his head. "We'll just have to keep our wits about us every minute, that's all," he said.

"You have the toughest job," Tom told him. "When you're out there playing football, you're taking a chance of getting bashed. Sitting in that wheelchair for me is easy. You know what?" he added quickly. "I've been realizing just what kind of life you really have been living, Mike. Being in that chair all the time ain't no picnic. It takes a lot of guts, man."

Michael's eyes flashed. "It takes guts to do what you do, too, Tom," he said seriously. "The team looks to you to make the plays work. I heard what they had to say when one doesn't! It's rough, a lot of pressure. It must be hard to stay on top all the time." Tom looked at him thoughtfully. "Sometimes," was all he said.

On October 4, the Eagles tangled with the Cheetahs. The day was sunny, and a light wind was blowing from the north, causing most of the fans to wear light jackets or sweaters.

The Cheetahs had a record of two wins and one loss, the same as the Eagles, so winning this game would mean a lot.

The Cheetahs won the toss and chose to receive. Vince's kick made the football veer off to the right of the field at the twenty-yard line, and it bounced out of bounds. He had to kick again, this time from the thirty-five-yard line. The kick, a high spiral, dropped near the twenty-five-yard line, where the receiver called for a free catch.

Kip Stanley, the Cheetahs' quarterback, hustled his team into a huddle and hustled them out of it. His eyes kept shifting over the field like a pair of white marbles as he barked signals. The ball was snapped, and he faded back. One step . . . two . . .

Abe Abrams, the Cheetahs' chunky fullback, took the handoff and plowed like a miniature tank through right tackle. Hands grabbed at him, but slipped off as if he were greased. He went twenty-three yards before Tom, playing safety, tackled him around the knees and pulled him down.

From his wheelchair, Michael looked on with disbelief. *What a run!* he thought. *If Kip is a smart quarterback, he'll try that play again.*

And Kip did! This time Abe chewed up eighteen yards before Angie, in the left linebacker position, brought him down.

You've got to sew up that hole, Tom! Michael's mind screamed. *You've got to sew it up, or Abrams will keep driving through it till he scores!*

Charlie Jarvis, the Cheetahs' left halfback, carried the ball next. Instead of trying to plow through right tackle, though, he sprinted around right end and got thrown for a two-yard loss.

Kip tried a pass that went incomplete. Then he tucked the ball into Abe's gut again, and Abe bulldozed into the line. He kept going, dodging the linebackers and then beating Tom to the goal line by just a step.

It was a touchdown.

Kip booted the ball between the uprights for the point after to put the Cheetahs on the scoreboard: 7–0.

Michael socked his knee with his fist. Less than two minutes had gone by and the Cheetahs had already drawn blood. The way they looked, and the way Abe Abrams was taking charge, that seven-point lead was sure to grow.

It did. And within the next two minutes, too.

The Cheetahs' tall, high-jumping right end, Don Falls, had snared a pass intended for Bob Riley and galloped all the way down the field for the Cheetahs' second touch-down. The try for the extra point was good, stretching the lead to 14–0.

Michael saw Tom standing as if in stunned surprise, his hands on his hips and his head lowered. He couldn't seem to believe that his first pass of the game could have been intercepted and then run for a touchdown.

Buck up, Tom! Michael tried to tell his brother through his extrasensory powers. *Don't let it get you down. It's still early in the game.*

The score remained 14–0 going into the second quarter. The ball was on the Eagles' forty-one-yard line. It was second and seven, Eagles' ball.

"Four! Six! Nine! Hip! Hip! Hip!" Tom barked.

He took the snap from center, fumbled it, picked it up, stumbled back.

Fumbled again! Luckily, Vince was right there to land on the ball, but the play went for a loss of yardage all the same.

C'mon, Tom, you're losing your concen-

tration out there! Let me in, and give your-self time to get your head together, Michael thought desperately. As if he had heard him, Tom shook his head.

But suddenly, the decision was taken out of both their hands.

"Kirk!" Coach Frank Cotter's voice boomed. "Get out there and take Tom's place!"

Kirk Tyler, the Eagles' backup quarter-back, pulled on his helmet as he sprinted out to the field.

Tom saw Kirk going in and started off the field, head down.

"I hope he's not too bummed out," a voice near Michael's elbow murmured.

He looked at the speaker. It was Vickie Marsh. Next to her stood the ever-present Carol Patterson.

"So do I," said Michael.

"Is Kirk any good?"

"I don't know. He'll be playing under pressure. That's the worst time."

As Tom approached, his eyes met Michael's. They looked tired and worried.

"Have a seat, Tom," Coach Patterson said. "You need a break."

If only he had let me give him that break! Michael thought dismally. *Then one of us would still be in the game.*

He caught Tom's eye again. The worried look was still there.

What are we going to do? Michael read Tom's thoughts. *Kirk isn't good enough to handle the team. I think you're better than he is, Michael. But are you strong enough to play for the rest of the game? And even if you are — how are you going to get in?*

It was the Eagles' ball on their own thirty-six-yard line. It was third down and twelve to go. Michael looked on helplessly as the team broke out of the huddle and trotted to the line of scrimmage. Some of the guys walked as if the spirit of playing had been drained out of them.

Kirk called signals, took the snap, and faded back to pass. He threw a long bomb to Stan down the left side of the field. But it sailed far over Stan's head, and was incomplete.

Vince punted on the fourth down and

managed to get the ball down near the Cheetahs' twenty-five-yard line.

Michael looked at Tom, saw him sitting with his helmet in his hands and his elbows on his knees. His hair was rumpled, and sticky with sweat.

We've got to do something, Tom. We can't just sit here like a couple of dummies.

But what else could they do? Michael wondered. He certainly couldn't just get out of his chair. And Tom was sitting on the bench, probably for the rest of the game.

Maybe, Michael reflected, the guys on the field had a lot to be dispirited about, at that.

But that was like giving up. And you cannot give up. Ever.

Out on the field the Cheetahs were moving again like a formidable herd. Charlie Jarvis had just bolted around left end for a first down.

"I think it's just terrible," Vickie said at Michael's elbow.

"What is?" asked Michael, startled briefly by the sound of her voice.

"Tom's being taken out, just because he made one or two mistakes."

"I think he should be able to get in again. That is, *I* think so," Michael said emphatically.

"I sure hope so," said Vickie.

"Come on, Vick," Carol broke in, grabbing her arm. "Let's get back to our seats. I'm getting tired standing."

"Okay. See you, Michael."

"Sure," said Michael.

He looked around at her a minute, wondering how she and Carol — as different as day and night — could get along so well together. Maybe it was what they needed, he thought; their differences made life interesting.

He turned his attention back to the game,

and noticed that Kip Stanley had just clicked with a pass to Chuck Philips for another first down. Oh, man.

The ball was now on the Eagles' forty-two-yard line. Wasn't there anything the Eagles could do to stop the rampaging Cheetahs?

Abe bolted through right tackle for four yards, then again for two.

"Button up that line!" Michael yelled. "Close it up tight!"

The linemen didn't hear him, of course. If they had heard, they didn't pay any attention to him. Maybe buttoning up the line would not help, anyway.

Then one of the Cheetahs was caught offside. The five-yard penalty helped the Eagles a little, but hardly enough. Abe made it up, and one extra yard, as he cross-bucked the line before Angie Costello brought him down.

Then, for a while, the Eagles held the Cheetahs and managed to get possession of the ball on the Eagles' twenty-four.

"Now, move it!" Coach Cotter yelled as he stood up from the bench, clapping hard. "Move it up that field! You can do it!"

They did it for eighteen yards, then lost the ball as Kirk heaved a sloppy pass that Kip intercepted. Kip made it to the Eagles' thirty-one, where Lumpy Harris hit him with one of his big shoulders, dropping him on the spot.

In just three plays the Cheetahs scored again, failing only to get the point after. Cheetahs 20, Eagles 0.

The half ended a few minutes later. Michael met Tom's eyes as Tom got off the bench to head with the pack down the field to the west goal, where they would sit and listen to Coach Cotter telling them what they had done wrong and what they had to do right. As if the guys didn't know, thought Michael despairingly.

"Tom, come here a minute," Michael called to his brother.

Tom came forward. "Yeah?"

"Think you can get back in?"

"I don't know. It's up to Coach. He's pretty steamed about that interception I threw, and that fumble didn't help, either. I'm not sure he's going to give me another chance — and I don't know if I even want one, tell you the truth. I'm afraid I'll do something worse if he does."

"Worse than what Kirk's doing out there now? C'mon, Tom, you and I both know that you're better than he is. And anyway, it's not just you the coach would be letting back in the game, right?"

Tom's eyes brightened as he looked at Michael hopefully.

"All you have to do, Tom, is convince the coach to sub you in again."

Tom's face fell. "How do I do that?"

Just then, Coach Cotter yelled for Tom to hustle on over.

"Leave it to me!" Michael said as Tom stood up. "Switch places with me after half-time and I'll coax Coach into putting me in."

Tom studied his brother for a moment, then gave a halfhearted shrug. "Okay. I gotta go now. See you in a bit."

Michael watched his brother's slumped shoulders as he joined the other Eagles. A sad look came into his eyes.

I wish Tom wouldn't doubt himself like that, he thought. *What'll it take to prove to him once and for all that he's a great quarterback?*

The third quarter began with Kirk still in the game. It was hardly under way when it became evident that the Cheetahs were on the move again. Although Kip's passes were not always on target, Abe Abrams's bucks through the line more than made up for the incompletions.

They were in Eagle territory, eating up yardage in big chunks, and the Eagles could not seem to do much about it.

Michael looked at Tom, but Tom was staring at his shoes.

Tom! Hey, Tom, for crying out loud! his

thoughts rang out almost as if they were audible.

Still Tom didn't turn around.

Then Michael began the other tack — wishing and concentrating on his thought-energies. Seconds went by — and then a minute — as he wished and concentrated harder and harder to make the exchange with Tom.

But, if Tom wasn't wishing and concentrating, too —

Suddenly, it happened! Michael was sitting on the bench in the exact spot where Tom had been sitting! On his left was Rick Howell, on his right, Coach Cotter. He glanced at Tom in the wheelchair, caught Tom's fleeting smile, and winked.

Good luck! Tom formed the words with his mouth.

His heart began to pound as he started to gather up courage to ask Coach Cotter to put him in the game. He could not waste much time.

On the field the Cheetahs had the ball on the Eagles' thirty-one-yard line. The down marker one of the linesmen was holding read two. There were about seven yards to go.

On the next play, Abe plowed through for two yards. Now it was third and five. A not-so-hard-to-get five the way the Cheetahs were going.

Then Kip took the snap and faded back to pass. Suddenly he went down, the ball squirting out of his hands. Somebody had gotten the jump on him. It was Lumpy! Good old Lumpy! Lumpy stayed on the ground, his arms wrapped around Kip like the strong jaws of a trap.

For a moment the ball bounced around freely. Then a guy in an Eagle's uniform pounced on it like a cat, smothering it. The whistle shrilled. It was the Eagles' ball!

Now was the time to go in, thought Michael. Now. While the guys were going into a huddle.

His lips trembled as he looked at the coach. "Coach, put me in there. I'm okay now. Please let me go in."

Coach Cotter looked at him. For a moment his eyes narrowed slightly, and fear sliced through Michael. He looked away, lifted his helmet, and started to put it on, hoping with all his might that the coach would just put him in without question.

"Are you sure your head is together now, Tom?" Coach asked. "You seem to have been drifting out there today."

"I know, Coach, but I'm sure you'll see an improvement in my playing." Michael finished putting the helmet on and faced the coach. "I — I'm a new man. I promise."

The coach crossed his arms and blew out

his breath. "Okay. Run in there. Hurry. And don't forget to send Kirk out."

Michael's heart leaped. "Thanks, Coach!" he cried, and dashed out on the field.

He reached the huddle just as it began to break up. "Sorry, Kirk," he said to the alternate quarterback.

Kirk looked at him. Without a word he spun and ran off the field.

"Huddle!" Michael commanded.

Quickly they got back into a huddle.

"T-forty-three drive," Michael snapped. "On three!"

In an instant they were out of the huddle and hurrying to the line of scrimmage. The ball was on the Eagles' thirty-seven.

Michael called signals. The ball was snapped. Michael took it, faked a handoff to Vince, then shoved the ball into Jim Berry's gut as he came running by. Jim plunged through for four yards.

"Power sweep left," said Michael in the huddle.

Vince stared at him. "You're going to run it?"

"We have to work on surprises from now on," Michael said tersely. "On two! Let's go!"

With Vince, Jim, and Angie cutting to the left side of the line, then blocking their men, Michael found his path around the left end clear sailing. The play caught the Cheetahs by surprise all right, for it was the first time that an Eagles quarterback had attempted a run since the start of the game. Michael crossed the fifty and just had one man between him and the goal line. That man was Kip, who doubled as quarterback and safety man, too, the same as Tom (or now, Michael) was doing.

Michael tried to sidestep Kip, but Kip dived at him and tackled him around the waist. He went down on the Cheetahs' twenty-eight.

Not since the game had started had the Eagles' fans cheered so loudly and lustily.

First and ten.

"Flat pass," said Michael in the huddle.

He got the snap, faded back, and shot a quick pass to Bob Riley in the flat to the right of the field. Bob sprinted for eight yards and was smeared.

Second and two.

"The same play," said Michael.

This time it didn't work. The pass was too short. It went incomplete.

Third and two.

"Let's try the drive again," said Michael.

They did, and the play went for five yards and another first down.

"T-forty-three," said Michael in the huddle.

Angie took the handoff and plowed through a hole on the right side for three yards. He ran again, and was stopped dead on the line of scrimmage.

"What now?" Vince asked, wiping the sweat off his forehead as they crouched in the huddle.

"You're driving again," Michael told him. "They'll be expecting a pass."

Michael took the snap from center, faded back as if to pass, then handed off to Vince. Vince went through a huge gap in the right side of the line, knocked over a linebacker, and bolted toward the right side of the end zone. He crossed it inches ahead of Kip, who had been about to tackle him, then had changed his mind.

Six points.

"Tired, Vince?" Michael asked him.

"Boy, am I," replied Vince, breathing hard.

"Okay. We'll pass," said Michael. No one disagreed.

Vince got into kicking position. Jack centered the ball to Michael. Michael started to put it down on the ground, then quickly lifted it to his shoulder and whipped it across the field to Stan. Nobody was near him, and he galloped down for a two-point conversion!

Cheetahs 20, Eagles 8.

Vince kicked off. Kip caught it on his thirty and went to the forty-two, where Butch Bogger nailed him.

Again the Cheetahs began their move. But only to the Eagles' forty-one. Again Lumpy's tackle caused Kip to lose the ball, and the Eagles recovered it.

In three plays the Eagles moved it to the Cheetahs' thirty-eight. Then the whistle shrilled, announcing the end of the third quarter. The teams changed goals.

Michael took off his helmet as he trotted across the fifty-yard line. Sweat beaded his forehead. Suddenly he realized that one of the guys had run up beside him. It was Vince.

"I don't know what happened on the sidelines, but it's like you're a different person since you got back in the game!" Vince said breathlessly.

The words hit Michael like a shot. Was the way he and Tom played so different? He wanted to know.

"What do you mean, Vince?" he asked.

Vince shrugged, his shoulder pads lifting. "I don't know, it's like you're more sure of yourself. You don't hesitate when you decide what play to run. Earlier this game, when we'd huddle up, you'd sort of look around to make sure we all agreed with what you'd called. Now you don't. The plays usually come off okay either way, but me and the guys kind of like it when you take charge. When you're confident in what you're doing, it makes us confident. I think we play better, too."

Somehow, Michael wasn't surprised by what Vince was saying. Tom's slumped shoulders at halftime had spoken volumes. He hadn't been confident in his playing in the two quarters of the game — and if what Vince was saying was true, then that attitude had affected the rest of the team.

As Michael lined up for the play, he realized that up until now, TEC had done two things for the twins: it had given Tom a chance to rest and Michael a chance to play. But now Michael saw that it could do one more thing. It could give Michael a chance to tell Tom what his teammates were thinking.

And what they were thinking was that

Tom was the best quarterback their team had. That they respected him and wanted him to be a leader.

And that's just what I'm going to let him be, Michael thought.

Michael broke into a faster trot. "Come on. Time's a-wastin'," he said.

The Eagles moved the ball to the Cheetahs' sixteen-yard line. Then a terrible thing happened. Abe Abrams busted through the line and tackled Michael for a twelve-yard loss. Not only that, but Michael fumbled the ball, too, and Abe recovered it!

"What lousy luck!" Vince cried, socking the air with his fist. "And we had them on the run!"

"Don't give up," said Michael, trying hard to keep cool over the loss. "Just don't give up."

In three plays the Cheetahs gained only six yards. They punted on the fourth. The kick went to their forty-six, where Michael grabbed it out of the air and carried it to the Cheetahs' thirty-one.

"We're almost back where we started from," he said happily in the huddle. "Okay. Flat pass to Bob."

The play succeeded for nineteen yards, putting the ball on the Cheetahs' twelve. On the next play Vince carried the ball through left tackle for their second touchdown. Then he booted it between the uprights to make it fifteen points against the Cheetahs' twenty.

"Another six points and we'll beat 'em," said Lumpy, grinning from a sweat-smeared face.

Vince chuckled. "Good adding, Lumpy. And you did it without a calculator, too."

"Smart mouth," snorted Lumpy.

Vince's kickoff was the poorest since the season had started. It was a bouncing kick that Charlie Jarvis snapped up on his own forty and carried to the Eagles' forty-three.

"Save that energy for your runs," said Michael, as Vince disgustedly kicked up sod with the toe of his shoe.

"Oh, sure," replied Vince. "As if we'll have another chance."

"We'll have another chance. We have to," Michael growled.

At that moment, Coach Cotter called a time-out. Michael rushed to the sidelines ahead of the rest of the team.

This is my chance! he thought wildly. *I've got to get to Tom and tell him what the team wants from him.*

He had no time to waste. As his team-mates gathered around the coach, he slipped onto the bench beside Tom in the wheelchair.

"Tom," he whispered urgently. "Listen closely. You're going back in the game."

Tom gave him a sharp look. "But you're playing so well —," he started to say.

"Cut it out!" Michael hissed. "I'm not playing any better than you usually do. There's only one difference: confidence. I've got it, and you need to get it, because that's what your teammates want from you."

"Tom!" Coach Cotter barked. "Get over here and listen up!"

Michael stood up but gave Tom one last meaningful look before he rejoined the team.

The horn blared, signaling the end of the time-out. Michael hesitated, waiting to feel the vibrations that indicated Tom was trying TEC. But no vibrations came.

Come on, Tom! Michael's mind called out. There was no reply.

Abe Abrams had the Cheetahs fired up as he led them down the field like an army on a triumphant march. Then, on the Eagles' four-yard line, they were stopped, and stopped cold. Three line plunges and a pass try failed to get them into the end zone.

"T-forty-three drive! On two!" Michael ordered in the huddle.

The play went for two yards. The Cheetahs, too, were holding.

Michael's forehead glistened with sweat as he faced the guys in the huddle.

"We've got to do it now or they'll break through when they get the ball," he said.

Suddenly, he felt the tingling. Tom was trying TEC! Michael immediately tuned in — and moments later found himself back in his wheelchair.

Okay, Tom, go for it! he urged silently.

As he watched, the huddle broke with a clap. Tom took the snap and stepped back into the pocket a couple of yards. Michael realized he was planning to throw a long bomb. Both ends were sprinting down the field, Bob at the left side, Stan at the right. Both were covered.

Then Stan buttonhooked in, and for a moment he was in the clear. Tom pulled his arm back and shot him a pass. The ball hit Stan in the gut, and Stan took it from there. He galloped down the field like a horse running a close race, and made it with yards to spare.

Cheetahs 20, Eagles 21! The Eagles were ahead by a point!

Moments later, the whistle blew. The game was over. The Eagles grabbed one another and cheered.

"One point, boy, that was close! But we won!" Jack cried, throwing his helmet into the air and catching it.

"Right!" said Lumpy.

"And you came through for us, Tom," Vince said, turning to the quarterback and pumping his hand vigorously. "You got us to tie up the score! Who would have thought a long bomb would work? But you called for it with such steel in your voice, I didn't even think about it. You're okay, man!"

Tom grinned through the sweat that streamed down his face. "Thanks, Vince. But it wasn't only me who did it." He glanced over at Michael and his grin broadened. "It was all of us."

Michael winked.

Suddenly a girl sprang in front of Tom and threw her arms around him, almost causing him to lose his balance and fall. It was Vickie, and Michael smiled. He wasn't surprised. For a long time she might have been waiting for an opportunity to throw her arms around Tom. What better time was there than now?

"Wasn't he great?" a voice broke in beside Michael. "You must sure be proud of him, Michael."

Michael glanced around at Carol, who was leaning against his wheelchair and resting a hand on it. Her dark eyes glistened as they met his, and before he knew it, she threw an arm around his neck and hugged him.

His heart pumped like crazy as she took her arm away and looked at Tom, a smile beaming on her face. *Wow!* Michael thought. *What a surprise! Whatever made me think she was a creep, anyway?*

Just then Michael saw a familiar figure coming toward them, a wide grin on his face.

"Nice game, boys," Ollie Pruitt said.

"Thanks, Mr. Pruitt," said Tom, and shook his hand.

Then Mr. Pruitt's eyes met Michael's,

and the old man winked. "How do you feel now, Michael?" he asked as they shook hands.

"Just great, Mr. Pruitt," Michael answered proudly. "Just great. Thanks to you."

READ ALL THE BOOKS

In The

New MATT CHRISTOPHER Sports Library!

THE BASKET COUNTS
978-1-59953-212-7

CATCH THAT PASS!
978-1-59953-105-2

CENTER COURT STING
978-1-59953-106-9

THE COMEBACK CHALLENGE
978-1-59953-211-0

DIRT BIKE RACER
978-1-59953-113-7

DIRT BIKE RUNAWAY
978-1-59953-215-8

THE GREAT QUARTERBACK SWITCH
978-1-59953-216-5

THE HOCKEY MACHINE
978-1-59953-214-1

ICE MAGIC
978-1-59953-112-0

THE KID WHO ONLY HIT HOMERS
978-1-59953-107-6

LONG-ARM QUARTERBACK
978-1-59953-114-4

MOUNTAIN BIKE MANIA
978-1-59953-108-3

RETURN OF THE HOME RUN KID
978-1-59953-213-4

SKATEBOARD TOUGH
978-1-59953-115-1

SNOWBOARD MAVERICK
978-1-59953-116-8

SNOWBOARD SHOWDOWN
978-1-59953-109-0

SOCCER HALFBACK
978-1-59953-110-6

SOCCER SCOOP
978-1-59953-117-5